Produced by Kroha Associates, Inc.
Middletown, Connecticut

Illustrated by Yakovetic Productions

Printed in the United States of America.

ISBN 1-56326-171-5

The Good Sport

The Little Mermaid loved playing finball with her friends, Flounder the fish and his sister Sandy. She would often brag to her sisters that the three of them were the best finball players in the sea. Then one day her sisters challenged them to a game. "I want to make sure we win the match," Ariel said to Sebastian the crab. "Will you help us practice?"

"Of course I will!" replied Sebastian. "I'll be your coach, and Scales will be my assistant!"

TWEEEET went Sebastian's whistle, and the practice began. Ariel, Flounder, and Sandy were playing against Scales. The dragon threw the ball to Sandy, but Flounder jumped in her way to hit the ball back over the net. "That was supposed to be for me!" said an annoyed Sandy.

"I didn't think you were ready," Flounder told her. "And besides, I'm really good at those tricky shots."

Then Scales threw the ball to the Little Mermaid. This time Flounder jumped in front of Ariel and hit the ball back over the net. "Flounder!" shouted Ariel. "That ball was supposed to be for me!"

"But I'm a much better hitter than you are," replied Flounder. "And we want to win, right?"

"We have to play together to win, Flounder," Ariel told him. "You're not the only one on this team."

"Ariel's right," said Sebastian. "You can't do it all by yourself."

"But I'm so much better than they are!" the little fish complained.

"You'd be even better if you worked with your teammates," advised Sebastian. "You have to let the others play, too."

Just then Ursula the evil sea witch came slithering around the corner with her pet eels. "What's this?" she cackled. "A little game of finball? Why, it's one of my favorite sports!"

"Really? Well, we're practicing for a match against Ariel's sisters," Sandy replied.

"Not that we need to practice — we're very good," Flounder said proudly.

"Is that so?" said the witch with a laugh. "Well, no matter how hard you practice, you and your little friends would never be able to beat me."

"Oh, yes we would!" Ariel said, defending her friends. "Our team is the best!"

"Well, then," replied the sea witch, "let's find out which team really is the best. What would you say to a little match — you and your friends against me and my eels, Flotsam and Jetsam? If you win, I'll do whatever you tell me to for three days. But if I win, each of you will have to do whatever I say for three whole weeks!"

Ariel whispered to Flounder, "Do you really think we can win?"

"Of course we can!" Flounder whispered back. "We're the best, remember?"

And so the game began. Ariel served the ball, and Flotsam slapped it back right at Sandy. Flounder leaped in front of his sister and batted the ball away, but Ursula, with her eight enormous tentacles, was right there to hit it back again and score the first point.

"Come on!" Scales cried from the sidelines. "You can do it!" But the shots the eels hit with their powerful tails were too much for Flounder to handle. He tried as hard as he could, leaping and diving and batting the ball, but it was no use. Ursula's team always scored the point.

TWEEET went Sebastian's whistle. "Time out!" he shouted. "I need to talk to my team!"

"Flounder, you keep trying to do everything by yourself!" Sebastian said as the three friends swam to meet him. "That's why we're losing."

"But I'm the best player we have!" Flounder objected. "If I let the others play, we'll only lose faster!"

"No one can do it all on his own," said Sebastian. "Everyone has something to contribute as part of the team. If the three of you work together, you'll be much stronger than any one of you could be playing alone. Try passing the ball to Ariel or Sandy. That way Ursula and her eels won't know who is really going to hit the ball over the net."

"Please, Flounder," Ariel pleaded. "We have to work together. After all, think of what's at stake — if we lose we have to do everything Ursula says for three weeks!"

Ursula served the ball right to Flounder. Flounder jumped up in the air, only this time instead of hitting the ball back at Ursula and her eels, he passed it to Sandy the way Sebastian had told him to. Flotsam and Jetsam were so confused, they got all tangled around each other.

Sandy easily knocked the ball over the net for a point. "Hooray!" cried Ariel. "It worked!"

Sebastian was right! Flounder realized. *The secret is teamwork!*

The three friends continued passing the ball back and forth, working together, which confused Ursula and her eels more and more. Soon the game was tied. The next team to score a point would be the winner.

"They're too good when they play together," Ursula told her eels. "We have to find a way to trick Flounder into trying to do it all on his own."

Ursula served the ball softly to Sandy, hoping that Flounder wouldn't be able to resist jumping in front of his sister to get the ball, just as he had so many times before. Then Ursula and her eels could gang up on Flounder and win the point.

Sure enough, Flounder did leap in front of Sandy for the ball. But instead of hitting it back over the net the way Ursula expected him to...

…he passed it to Ariel, who easily smashed the ball over the net for the winning point!

"Hooray!" Scales shouted, jumping up and down with glee. "Our team won!"

"I knew they could do it," said Sebastian proudly. "Now we're *really* ready for the match with Ariel's sisters."

"Wait!" cried the sea witch as she tried to untangle herself from her eels. "You cheated!"

"No we didn't," replied Flounder. "We just used teamwork."

"Now you'll do what we want for three days," Ariel reminded Ursula. "And we'll be wanting lots of seaberry muffins!"